THE LIGHT CHASER MYSTERIES

2

MYSTERIOUS SIGNS

HORIZON BOOKS
CAMP HILL, PENNSYLVANIA

Dedicated to
Jim & Koleen

Horizon Books
3825 Hartzdale Drive
Camp Hill, PA 17011

ISBN: 0-88965-107-8
LOC Catalog Card Number: 93-74958
© 1994 by Mark Weinrich
All rights reserved
Printed in the United States of America

Cover art © by Gary Watson

94 95 96 97 98   5   4   3   2   1

Book 2 of the Light Chaser Mystery Series

Mysterious Signs

1

Scared Silly

"Rainie, we'd better turn back," Denise Rodriquez said as she pointed at the ominous purple clouds to the west.

Rainie turned and looked at the clouds and then kept climbing up the hill. She was tired of Denise's endless chatter. Why'd she have to come along?

"That storm is going to hit in a few minutes," nagged Denise.

"Quit worrying, Denise. We're almost to the top." At least, Rainie hoped they were almost there, because it seemed that the hill kept growing before them. Vick's Peak was still hidden by the hill and the day kept getting darker.

Rainie, Denise, Rainie's brother Ryan and Ryan's friend Carl McDaniel had been hiking all morning and afternoon, but they hadn't found even one exciting thing.

Rainie knew Ryan was still mad about last night. They'd fought over where they were going today. He'd seen lights on the slopes below Vick's Peak and wanted to investigate. But she wanted to solve the meaning of the petroglyph.

A petroglyph is a picture or pattern etched in stone. Early Indians had etched a strange pattern high on a wall in Monticello Canyon. Rainie wanted to figure out why it was there, because an archaeologist was going to be speaking at the museum in Geronimo Springs a week from Thursday. That was less than two weeks away. Rainie felt sure the petroglyph would lead to an important discovery, and she wanted to have time to talk it over with an expert. But Ryan had his own ideas. He wanted to solve a mystery on his own.

Uncle Matt had almost canceled their exploring plans, until they compromised. Ryan would help Rainie solve her mystery today and then Rainie would help Ryan the next day. And that's where Denise came in. Denise was sixteen, only three years older than Rainie. Uncle Matt had insisted that Denise go along because she was experienced with the horses. She lived on the next ranch above Uncle Matt's.

"Wait up," Denise yelled.

Rainie stopped for an instant and looked back. She was surprised how far Denise was behind. Denise had been taking pictures again. Rainie couldn't believe how many shots Denise had taken already that day. At least it wasn't as annoying as her chatter.

Rainie glanced farther down the slope. Ryan and Carl looked like specks as they searched the grassy level below. Rainie caught her breath and started upward again.

"Wait up," Denise yelled again.

The grass got thinner the higher Rainie climbed. Now, red broken rocks stuck out of the slope. They clinked like glass as she almost slipped and fell. It was getting too dark to see all the rocks.

Then she remembered the sunglasses. Uncle Matt had given them to her that morning. She slipped them off and put them in her shirt pocket. That was better. Now the clouds didn't look as threatening.

Rainie was almost to the ridgeline when Denise yelled again. Now what, she thought.

"I think Ryan and Carl have found something."

"Are you sure?" Rainie yelled.

"They're jumping up and down and waving, but I can't tell what they're saying."

Rainie started down. Denise was taking a picture of the storm clouds when Rainie reached her.

Denise put her camera back in the case that hung around her neck. "We'd better find out what they've found and then get back to the horses."

"I guess you're right," Rainie said. "But I hate to leave when we're so close to the top."

"Have you ever been in a flash flood?"

"No, but Uncle Matt told me about them."

"If we don't get down from here now we might get caught in one," stated Denise.

Rainie resented the way Denise tried to run things. This morning when Rainie had wanted to climb up the wall with the petroglyph on it, Denise wouldn't let her. Later, after they had taken the long way around, Rainie figured out why Denise wouldn't climb the wall. Denise was afraid of heights.

As Rainie had leaned out over the ledge to make sure she was right above the petroglyph, Denise panicked. She grabbed Rainie and almost dragged her from the ledge. Rainie thought Denise was trying to push her over. Both teetered dangerously near the edge.

She had yelled at Denise to leave her alone. Rainie regretted that now. She felt bad about losing her temper.

"Denise, I'm sorry about yelling at you this morning. I know you just wanted to help me."

"I guess I should've been honest with you and told you I'm afraid of heights," Denise replied.

Both were silent. They crossed the two track road where Rainie had solved the mystery of the vanishing lights the week before. Two weeks of their vacation had already passed. It seemed like only yesterday since Ryan and Rainie had come to New Mexico to visit Uncle Matt and Aunt Amie at their Warm Springs Ranch. Ten days ago Val and Cinch, Uncle Matt's ranch hands, had taught them to ride horses. Now Rainie felt like ranch life was the kind of life she was meant to live.

"Hey, we've found something!" Ryan yelled.

The boys stood a hundred yards away with their heads bowed. They were looking at something on the ground. Rainie thought they were too far south of the petroglyph for it to be anything connected with that. She had walked straight up the hill from the petroglyph because she thought something might be on the hilltop. Since the petroglyph looked like a Mayan or Aztec step pyramid, maybe there was something on top. She walked slowly, disappointed that she'd had to turn back.

"I'm sorry that I've been such a chatterbox," Denise said. "When I'm around new people I just lose it. I get so nervous I just can't help myself."

"That's all right," Rainie said. "I've been mad at Ryan because he wouldn't agree to do things my way. I think I've probably taken things out on you."

"Hurry up," Ryan called.

The girls jogged the last several hundred feet to meet the boys.

"It's some kind of wheel," Carl said.

"How would a wheel get up here?" Ryan asked.

"There's a road over there," Rainie said. "Remember?"

"You're just sore because we found it and you didn't," Ryan said.

"This doesn't have anything to do with the petroglyph," Rainie said. "It's modern."

"Look here." Denise pointed to an area behind

the wheel where about six feet of grass had been
crushed.

"So what?" Ryan asked.

"I think it's an airplane wheel," Denise said.

"An airplane wheel!" Carl exclaimed.

"Someone must have tried to land up here,"
Rainie said.

"Listen," Ryan said.

They looked at each other and then up the hill. A
black helicopter flew over the hill. The unmarked
helicopter looked like a giant black hornet. It flew
toward them and then hovered over them. Its
deafening beating sound made them hold their
ears.

Rainie felt like her heart was going to burst.
After a few seconds, the helicopter started to des-
cend. They ran as though being chased by a
swarm of bees.

Ryan led them toward a bush at the head of an
arroyo. He jumped into the arroyo and the others
followed.

Rainie stopped. Why were they running? They
hadn't done anything wrong. She turned around
in time to see two men in camouflaged uniforms
emerge from the open door. One had a rifle slung
over his shoulder. They picked up the wheel and
threw it in the open door. They jumped back in
and slid the door shut. The helicopter hovered
momentarily then spun quickly and returned the
same way it came.

2

Cut Off

"**W**here are you going?" Ryan yelled as he peeked from the bush at the head of the arroyo.

"I'm going to see where the helicopter landed," Rainie said.

"Wait," Ryan called. "What if they come back?"

"I don't think they're coming back," Rainie said. "They took the wheel."

"They what?" Ryan stepped from behind the bush. Denise and Carl followed.

"If you hadn't been so scared, you would've seen them," Rainie replied.

"You ran, too!" Ryan exclaimed.

"But I stopped long enough to watch." Rainie turned and walked to where the helicopter had landed. She inspected the ground. The grass was crushed where the helicopter had set down. A

raindrop hit her cheek. Just as she turned to join
the others, she noticed something black not far
from where the wheel had been.

"Rainie, come on," Denise yelled.

Before Rainie had a chance to respond, the sky
opened up. Raindrops chattered as they exploded
in the grass.

Rainie grabbed the black object. It was about the
size of a TV remote control with a short rubber an-
tenna. She thought it was some kind of radio. She
hurriedly found the controls, turned on the power
and adjusted the volume.

A man's voice came from the radio, "It must have
been going northeast when it went down. We're
headed back. Over." Then the radio was silent.

"Come on!" Ryan yelled.

She ran after the others.

They disappeared into the arroyo as soon as
Rainie started toward them.

Water was already flowing in a small stream
down the arroyo when Rainie reached the bush.
She had no choice but to slop through it. Now she
was worried. It would be all her fault if they were
cut off by a flash flood. She should have listened to
Denise and turned back earlier. *Lord*, she prayed,
please don't let us be cut off.

Water trickled off the bill of Rainie's cap. With a
downpour like this it did not take long for her to
feel soaked through. The rain felt warm, but what
about the radio? Would water hurt it? She pulled
out her shirttail and put the radio under her shirt

and held it tight against her stomach.

She looked down the arroyo. It curved back and forth from the mesa top to the valley where hundreds of years of rain had cut through the hillside. Boulders and old tree roots stuck out of the arroyo banks. The arroyo floor was a jumble of different sizes and shapes of boulders.

Rainie zigzagged around and over boulder after boulder. The polished surface of the boulders made the footing slippery. She fell twice when her feet slipped out from under her. She stopped and put the radio in the waistband of her jeans so she could use both hands.

Now the water ran ankle deep. She was really worried. Where were the others? Had she missed them?

Then she heard a sound from the canyon. At first just a muffled rumble, then as she rounded the last turn she saw Ryan. Ryan, Carl and Denise were huddled together under a stunted oak watching the muddy waters rush down the canyon.

Her heart sank. They were cut off. The churning brown waters sounded almost like a waterfall, but more like the roar of crashing waves against rocks at the ocean. Rainie saw Carl point at a geyser of mud as the flood waters collided with a tree trunk below them.

The others didn't notice her approach. The rain was now just a drizzle.

"How long have you been waiting?" Rainie asked.

Denise turned and said, "About five minutes."

"You should have seen the five foot wall of water that just passed," Ryan said.

"We should have been on the other side," Carl added.

Rainie looked away to avoid their angry eyes. "What are we going to do?"

"We'll have to climb back up and go back the way we came," Carl said. "Then we'll see if we can get back to the horses."

"Will they be all right?" Rainie asked.

"They're probably fine," Carl said. "I'm just glad Denise had us tie them where we did."

Rainie held her breath. What was wrong with her? She hadn't even thought about the horses before Carl mentioned them. They had left the horses on a grassy bench just above the creekbed. She looked at Carl, "You're sure they're okay?"

"The water gets pretty high in this canyon but not that high."

She breathed a sigh of relief.

"How high does it get?" Ryan asked.

"About fifteen feet where it passes below our house." Then Carl pointed at the muddy creek in front of them, "It's already about five or six feet deep right here."

"Can we cross it?" Rainie asked.

"Are you kidding?" Ryan said.

"It would be like stepping in front of a moving train," Denise said.

"What's that under your shirt?" Ryan asked.

Rainie had forgotten the radio. She pulled it out.

"Where'd you get that?" Denise asked.

"One of those guys from the helicopter must have lost it when he bent over to pick up the airplane wheel," said Rainie.

"How do you know it was an airplane wheel?" Carl asked.

Rainie told them about what she'd heard on the radio.

"Maybe we should call them for help?" Denise said.

"We don't know who or what they are," Rainie cautioned. "And besides that, one of them was carrying a rifle." She stuck the radio back in her waistband.

It started raining hard again. "We'd better get back to the horses," Denise said. "Our folks are going to be worried about us."

Rainie looked at Carl. "Will we be able to find a place to cross?"

"Maybe," Carl said. "I think I have an idea."

3

Tightrope Act

The rain had stopped when they finally saw the horses on the bench below them.

"Praise the Lord," Ryan said. "The horses are still there."

Rainie thought Ryan was starting to sound a lot like Uncle Matt. It was wonderful how Ryan had changed since he accepted Jesus as his Savior. But Rainie felt like she was going backward. Why had she been fighting with Ryan like she did before he became a Christian? Why had she treated Denise so poorly? Why hadn't God answered her prayer? Now, they were cut off by the flood. She knew and believed God could control the waters; so why didn't He? Now all this mess was her fault.

"We'll have to strip the horses and cover the saddles and blankets," Carl said. "There're rain slickers tied to the back of the saddles. We can cover everything with them."

"Why can't we take the horses?" Rainie asked.

"They won't cross the creek when it's this high," Carl said. "Besides, they won't be able to cross the way we're going to cross."

"How are we going to cross?" Rainie asked.

"I'll show you in a minute," Carl said as he and Ryan went to get the horses.

"Rainie, I forgot to tell you. I got a couple of shots of that helicopter as it turned and took off," Denise said as she took her camera from around her neck.

"Great," Rainie said. "That's the best news I've had all day." She took the radio and laid it next to Denise's camera.

Rainie patted her shirt pocket for her sunglasses. They weren't there. "Has anyone seen my sunglasses?"

"Your sunglasses?" Ryan questioned as he passed the reins of Rainie's horse to her. "They're Uncle Matt's."

"I know," Rainie said. "But I can't picture Uncle Matt wearing them. I guess I must have lost them in the arroyo when I fell." What else could go wrong, Rainie thought. How would she tell Uncle Matt?

"We should have seen them when we came back up," Denise said.

"Maybe I lost them when I ran to catch up with you after I found the radio."

After they stripped the horses, they covered the saddles and blankets with the slickers and then weighted it all down with rocks.

"Now we'll see if we can get out of here," Carl said as he picked up his lariat. "We need to get over to that boulder." He pointed down the canyon to a narrow gap where a large boulder jutted out into the flood-swollen creek.

"How are we going to do that?" Rainie asked. "There's no longer any bank to walk along."

"We'll have to cross the slope and then crawl down to the boulder," Carl said.

"That's crazy," Denise said.

Rainie thought of Denise's fear of heights. "You're sure there's no other way?"

"Not unless you want to camp here," Carl said.

"That wouldn't be too bad," Denise said.

"How long could we be stuck here?" Rainie asked.

"No telling," Carl said, "maybe a couple days or a week. Two years ago we were stuck at our house for ten days."

"I'm for climbing," Ryan said.

"Denise, I don't think we have any choice," Rainie said.

"We can use the rope if we have to," Ryan said.

Rainie felt terrible when she saw the sick look on Denise's face. She would never forgive herself if anything happened to Denise.

"Maybe we could tie you between us," Carl said as he held up the lariat to Denise. Then he tied one end around Ryan's waist. "Can we try?" he asked Denise.

Denise nodded yes.

"Let's pray before we try anything," Rainie said. She prayed for their protection and for safety as they crossed the slope.

Denise didn't say a thing as Carl tied the middle of the rope around her and then the end to himself. Rainie saw that Denise was trembling as they started across the slope. Carl led out and Rainie followed holding tightly to Ryan's hand.

Denise had been fine the other times going up and down the arroyo, Rainie thought, but that was like going up and down a staircase. Rainie prayed again.

Carl and Ryan kept the rope taut and traveled at Denise's pace. Rainie was proud of Ryan. He didn't complain once about their slow progress across and then up the slope. Carl led them where they could grab rocks or brush.

Carl waited on a large flat rock and took in the rope as Denise climbed up the rock. When they were all on the rock, he said, "We'll rest for a little while and then we'll start."

The boulder was diagonally down from them now. It looked easier here than where they'd just come.

Carl led out again, but Denise slipped before Ryan had even left the flat rock. Rainie grabbed Ryan's belt from behind and stopped him from being pulled off the rock.

"There are fewer handholds down here," Carl yelled.

"Are you all right, Denise?" Rainie called.

Ryan moved down next to Denise. "Here let me get a firm footing, then I'll let you down," he offered.

Denise inched down. She trembled like she was shivering from being cold.

Now Rainie was on her own. She was glad for the slow pace.

"We're almost there," Carl called.

The boulder was connected to the hillside by a saddle of dirt and rock. The flood tore at the bottom of the saddle. Big blotches of mud splashed against the boulder. Carl put one foot down on the saddle and tested it. "It's safe," he called and crawled onto the boulder.

When Denise reached the boulder she hugged Carl and smiled. "I did it," she said. "Thank you. I did it."

Ryan gave Carl a high-five when he reached the boulder and Denise welcomed Rainie with a hug.

"That was the easy part," Carl said.

Denise's smile disappeared.

Carl untied the rope and coiled it. He made a loop, then threw it and caught a large broken branch of a cottonwood on the other creek bank. "If that snag holds we might get home before dark."

"What are we going to do?" Rainie asked.

"We're going to walk across it," Ryan said with a big smile.

"Help me," Carl said to Ryan. They both pulled

with all their weight against the broken branch. "It'll hold us," Carl announced.

"Hold us," Denise protested. "I don't know that I . . ."

"Just watch," Carl said. He passed the rope through a crack in the boulder and wedged a large rock across the crack. Then he tied the rope around the rock. "How long has it been since you crossed monkey bars?" Carl asked.

No one responded.

Carl edged backward out onto the rope. He grasped the rope tightly and then let his legs dangle. The water rushed only inches from his feet. He pulled his legs back up and hooked the inside of his knees across the rope. Working arm over arm he pulled himself across and then dropped to the bank on the other side.

"Denise, it's your turn," he called.

"You can do it," Rainie said.

Denise wasn't trembling this time, but she had that sick look on her face again.

"Throw your camera across," Carl called.

"I'll do it," Ryan said. He threw the camera to Carl.

"Wait," Rainie said. She handed the radio to Ryan and he threw it across, too.

Denise backed out onto the rope like Carl and let her legs down. She panicked when her feet barely touched the water. "I can't do it. I can't!" she screamed.

"Pull your legs up!" Ryan yelled. "Pull!"

Denise moved her hands and got a better hold and then swung her legs over the rope. She inched her way across with her eyes closed.

"You can drop now," Carl yelled. He grabbed her as she dropped and pulled her safely to the bank.

After Rainie and Ryan crossed, Carl said, "Once we find the right ridge, we can take the mesa top and then drop down behind our house."

They walked into a grove of low-growing black walnut trees; water flowed ankle deep along the ground.

"What's that sound?" Rainie asked. The sound of the creek behind them had stopped. Now they heard the splashing of water in front of them.

"We're going the wrong way," Carl said.

"How can you tell?" Ryan asked.

"I'm pretty sure that we're near the Bath," Carl said.

"The what?" Rainie asked.

"It's a rock formation shaped like a bathtub. It's at the end of an arroyo. That's probably the sound of a waterfall."

"Why don't we go look at it?" Rainie said.

"We need to go south from here and climb the other ridge."

"How hard a climb will it be?" Denise asked.

The others laughed.

"It won't be hard," Carl said. "But wait, I just remembered something."

"What?" Denise asked, her voice sounding concerned.

"If we get to the Bath fast, we might be able to get back home before dark," Carl said.

Carl led them deeper into the grove of trees, but they had to turn north because the water flowed almost knee deep. They walked up a small ridge to where they could see the waterfall. Hundreds of years of water action had sculpted the arroyo end into a crudely shaped bathtub.

"Is that what you wanted us to see?" Rainie asked. A twelve foot muddy waterfall flowed before them.

"No," Carl said. "My dad showed me some petroglyphs here one time."

"Where?" Rainie asked.

"They're on this side just below us."

"If we edge our way along the water line, could we see them?" Rainie asked.

"I think we could."

"I'll wait here," Denise said.

"I'll keep her company," Ryan added.

Carl led Rainie down toward the water edge. They grabbed overhanging brush and balanced on rocks.

"Can you see the drawing of a deer?" Carl asked.

"Yes," Rainie said as she pointed to another petroglyph. "Is that what you wanted me to see?"

Carl nodded. They both looked at the three-step pyramid.

"It must have something to do with the other one," Rainie said, excitement filling her voice.

4

Geronimo's Gold

$\mathcal{T}$he circle of the yardlight caught their shadows when the kids walked into the ranch yard just after dark. The ranch dogs rushed out to announce their return. Mr. and Mrs. McDaniel and Carl's little brother and sister ran out of the house to greet them.

Rainie was so tired and weary she wanted to drop anywhere dry so she could sleep and sleep. But once the smell of beans and tortillas reached her, she realized she was famished. Then she remembered Uncle Matt and Aunt Amie. She'd call them first and let them know they were okay.

During supper, Rainie, Ryan and Denise told how Carl had led them back. Denise even laughed about her day's terrifying events.

While the others told the McDaniels about the airplane wheel, the helicopter, and showed them the radio, Rainie was silent. She felt like she was sick, because she knew it had all been her fault. If she had just listened to Denise and turned back right away, nothing would have happened. She thanked the Lord for His protection, but that still didn't take away her uneasy feeling.

"You kids better stay away from that area for a while," Mr. McDaniel said.

"Why?" Ryan asked.

"There's a drug smuggler's airstrip about five miles above that petroglyph. There have been two plane crashes in that area in the last few years."

"Maybe it wasn't a drug smuggler's plane," Carl suggested.

"If it had been a private plane," Mr. McDaniel said, "we would've heard something over the news about a missing plane."

"That explains the mountain lights!" Ryan said. "The drug smugglers are trying to find their plane."

"But what about the helicopter?" Rainie asked. "If the drug smugglers owned one, they wouldn't need to fly drugs across the border in planes."

"You're probably right," Mr. McDaniel said. "It could be the Border Patrol's or the Drug Enforcement Agency's. But I wouldn't eliminate the drug smugglers totally. Theirs is a multimillion dollar business."

"We could still try to find out why the petroglyphs are there, couldn't we?" Rainie asked.

"As far as I'm concerned you can look for

Geronimo's gold," Mr. McDaniel said with a smile. "But you stay a good distance away from that airstrip."

"Geronimo's gold!" Ryan exclaimed. "What's that?"

Oh no, Rainie thought, now Ryan has another mystery. Ever since he'd seen the lights on the San Mateo Mountains, he'd wanted to solve a mystery of his own.

"I thought Rainie would have told you that story," Mr. McDaniel said.

Rainie swallowed hard.

Ryan looked at Rainie with accusing eyes.

"It wasn't important," Rainie said. "Besides it's just a story."

"Some people think it's true," Mrs. McDaniel said as she started clearing the table.

Rainie got up to help her. She knew if Ryan heard about another mystery to try and solve she would never figure out the petroglyph mystery before the archaeologist came.

"Well, tell me," Ryan said.

"After John Clum caught Geronimo," Mr. McDaniel explained, "Geronimo was confined in a room in Fort Ojo Caliente. He told John Clum that if he would release him he would fill the room with gold in a day's time."

"Wow!" Ryan gasped.

"Because of that story many think there is an Apache gold mine somewhere in this area," Mr. McDaniel explained.

Rainie had never thought about the full impact of the story, until she saw Ryan's reaction. He sat on his knees on his chair and leaned over the table on his elbows as close as he could get to Mr. McDaniel.

"Can we look for it?" Ryan asked.

"As long as you stay away from the airstrip," Mr. McDaniel said. "Until someone finds that plane, I don't want you to take a chance of running into those smugglers. You have no idea what they might do to you if they thought you had any information about that plane crash."

"What about the radio?" Ryan asked.

"Let me look at it again," Mr. McDaniel said.

Rainie got the radio and gave it to Mr. McDaniel. He tried the buttons on the front and the knobs on the top. "I think the batteries have run down. The power knob was left on."

"It started raining when I heard the message," Rainie said. "I don't remember if I turned it off."

"That's all right. We can get more batteries for it," Mr. McDaniel said. "I was trying to see if there was any identification on it." He slipped the back off and looked at the batteries. Then he took out ten batteries.

"Why would it need so many batteries?" Rainie asked.

"I'd say this is an expensive and powerful radio. It probably needs those because it can transmit and receive from a long ways off."

"We need to find places for them to sleep," Mrs.

McDaniel interrupted. "They've had a long and tiring day."

No one complained.

While Mrs. McDaniel scurried around making up beds, the rest of the group decided to take another look at the flood.

The McDaniel Ranch headquarters was spread across a bench that stuck out into the valley like a thumb. A dike had been built below the bench to keep the water from flowing into the ranch corrals and hay fields, but the flood waters had overflowed now and ran through the corrals.

"The corrals are down there," Carl pointed.

The ugly brown water flowed like a runaway train about ten feet below where Mr. McDaniel and the kids stood.

"How deep is it?" Rainie asked.

"At least twenty feet," Mr. McDaniel said. "The dike is fourteen feet high and the corral posts are five feet tall."

They couldn't see the corral posts. The creek had become an angry river mowing down anything in its path.

Rainie saw the road rising out of the river on a hill in the distance. They were cut off, trapped. At least, Rainie felt trapped. There were now only ten days left until the archaeologist was going to be in Geronimo Springs. And she still didn't have any answers.

"Do you have a rubber raft?" Ryan asked Carl.

"Why?" Carl replied with a puzzled look on his face.

"We could go brown-water rafting," Ryan joked. Carl and Mr. McDaniel laughed with Ryan.

Rainie didn't think it was funny because she knew the McDaniels had been trapped for as many as ten days in the past.

5

The Raven and the Dove

When the waters finally receded two days later, Rainie, Ryan, Carl and Denise were ready to search for the horses. The smell of rain still hung heavy in the air as Mr. McDaniel drove them back up Monticello Canyon. The sun barely peeked over the eastern ridge.

Ryan and Carl rode in the back of the pickup and Rainie and Denise rode in the cab. But much of the time Ryan and Carl walked ahead of the truck removing rocks and large limbs from the road. Rainie couldn't remember experiencing a rougher ride. They bounced along at little more than a crawl.

"The county grader will have to fix the road before anyone else will be able to travel this way,"

Mr. McDaniel said. Glancing at Denise, he continued, "You'll have to take the long way home
this afternoon."

Darkness lingered in the canyon narrows and it
smelled musty like a basement or a cave. Only the
joyous chatter of some rock squirrels broke the
morning's gloomy feeling.

Twice trees blocked the road. Mr. McDaniel used
a chain and the pickup to pull them to the side of
the road so they could pass.

Decaying remains from the flood hung
everywhere as they advanced up the canyon.
Grass and great clumps of mud were wrapped
around the trunks of cottonwood trees. From the
canyon to the canopy of the cottonwood trees
muddy debris was wedged against all the rocks
and trees. The thin willows that lined the creek
were flattened.

"It looks like some giant beavers have been at
work," Rainie said. Branches, grass, boulders and
trees were intertwined like beaver dams and
jammed together on the sides of the canyon.

"And then some giant fist smashed through the
middle," Denise added.

"Those giant beavers sure did a job on my corrals," Mr. McDaniel said.

"I'm sure my dad will be down in a few days to
help you fix your corrals," Denise said.

"Maybe Uncle Matt and Val or Cinch could help
too," Rainie suggested.

"Thanks," Mr. McDaniel said, "but there are

ranches further down canyon that had a lot worse damage than we suffered. We'll probably start down there and work up to my ranch."

Rainie still couldn't get over the destruction of the flood. The McDaniels' corrals had been broken off at ground level in most places, like a giant fist had grabbed hold of the posts and broken them like toothpicks.

"Did you figure anything out from the maps I gave you?" Mr. McDaniel asked.

"I've got an idea," Rainie said, "but I'm not sure about it yet."

Since their narrow escape from the flood on Saturday, Rainie had spent much of the past two days looking at the maps that Mr. McDaniel had of the ranch and the surrounding area. She had never felt so frustrated. There was so little time and no way to figure anything out. At least the maps offered something to keep her mind busy.

It was hard to believe that it was already Tuesday. On Sunday morning, Mr. McDaniel had led his family and the kids in a short service. Rainie was still bothered by some things she had learned—things she had learned about herself.

During the service in the family living room, Mr. McDaniel thanked the Lord for protecting the kids and for His provision of a safe warm place to wait out the flood. Then he commented that there had been eight people who were saved on Noah's ark and there were eight people who had been protected from the flood now.

As he discussed how God led Noah and his family through the flood, Carrie, Carl's sister asked a question: "Why did the dove come back and not the raven? What happened to the raven?"

"Do you really want to know?" Mr. McDaniel asked.

Carrie nodded.

"It's not very pretty," Mr. McDaniel said.

Now Rainie was really interested, too. She had never thought about what happened to the raven.

"Carrie, what happens when a rabbit gets hit on the road?" Mr. McDaniel asked.

"The ravens wait by the road and try to eat it," she said.

"Imagine all the people and animals that died in the flood," Mr. McDaniel said. "What did the raven find?"

"Yuck," Carrie said and shook her head. "But why did the dove come back?"

"Can you imagine how it smelled," Ryan interrupted holding his nose.

Carl laughed with Ryan.

"You're right," Mr. McDaniel said. "The dove could find nothing to eat the first time because the world was a terrible smelly mess."

"And that's the way our lives are, kids, when we try to live the Christian life on our own," Mrs. McDaniel added.

"What do you mean?" Rainie asked.

"We make a terrible mess of our lives when we try to live them on our own," Mrs. McDaniel said.

"I once heard a preacher say, the dove and the raven illustrate two ways Christians try to live their lives. The dove represents those who want to live God's way—living by His Holy Spirit. The raven represents those who live their life on their own."

Rainie. felt terrible when she heard Mrs. McDaniel's words. She knew that she had been living her life on her own, like the raven, for the past few days. Ryan, Carl, and Denise had been good about not blaming her for all that had happened. She deserved it. If she hadn't been so tied up in her mystery. . . . If she'd only turned back earlier. . . .

For the rest of Sunday and Monday, Denise, Ryan and Carl played board games; except once when Ryan and Carl looked up San Mateo Canyon on the maps. That was where Geronimo's gold was supposed to be hidden. Rainie didn't know what they expected to find. She still examined the maps closely trying to figure out her mystery.

She had formed an idea about the petroglyphs. Since each had equal steps on both sides maybe they pointed to something on the hilltops. If Ryan hadn't found the airplane wheel she might have figured out what was above the five-step pyramid. But then again the rain had spoiled everything. And it was her fault that they had been caught in the flash flood. Why did everything have to be so frustrating and confusing now? Maybe she should help Ryan try to find Geronimo's gold.

As they drove further up the canyon, they all looked on the eastern slopes for the horses. The western slopes were clear and bright; every fold and break of the ridges stuck out as though one were looking through binoculars. But the eastern slopes were hidden in shadows. Rainie didn't know how they could see anything, but in the dim light Denise pointed out a lone mule deer doe grazing on the eastern slope above them.

The walls narrowed again. There was no way to see the slopes on either side. Where the canyon opened up again, Rainie noticed a hill rising on the left. Tingles went up her back. She felt excited for the first time in days.

"Is the Bath near here?" Rainie asked.

"See the break close to the bottom of that hill," Mr. McDaniel said. He pointed at the hill that had caught Rainie's attention.

"Could we stop for a minute?" Rainie asked.

"Sure," Mr. McDaniel said. "But why?"

"Would you take a picture of that hill, please?" Rainie asked Denise.

Mr. McDaniel stopped the truck.

"Why?" Denise asked as she opened her camera case.

"I've got an idea," Rainie said. "It has to do with the petroglyph in the Bath."

Denise stepped in front of the truck and snapped the picture.

"Could I check something on that hill while you look for the horses?" Rainie asked.

"I don't see any problem with it as long as some-one goes with you," Mr. McDaniel said. "The boys and I can find the horses, but we'll need you to help ride them back."

"Okay, great," said Rainie. "We'll see you later." She turned around and discovered that Denise didn't look pleased.

6

Stranded

Denise shoved the camera in her case and snapped it shut.

"You'll go with me?" Rainie asked.

"It looks pretty steep."

"We'll try to find the easiest way up," Rainie assured her.

"The saddles and blankets are over there," Carl called from the back of the pickup. He pointed across the creek.

"We can walk from here," Rainie said as Mr. McDaniel started the truck.

"If you get down before we find the horses," Mr. McDaniel said, "just wait at the bottom of the hill." Then he reached behind the seat and grabbed a canteen. "Here. Take this."

Rainie and Denise walked up the road and entered a grove of black walnut trees. They ducked often avoiding low hanging limbs as they worked their way to the bottom of the hill.

Rainie noticed a trail that ran up the hill beside a large boulder. "Let's go look at the Bath again," she said.

They passed to the left of the boulder and the Bath opened before them. There was no muddy colored waterfall now, only a brown polished rock formation shaped like the end of a bathtub. The petroglyph was on the right wall.

Rainie saw other shapes and figures next to the three-step pyramid, but they were faded beyond recognition. Higher up, almost at the top level of the waterfall, an animal figure looked like it was running up the wall. At one time there must have been many other petroglyphs, but the rock had weathered and crumbled.

Denise took another picture of the pyramid. "The light's better now than it was the other day."

"Let's try and go up the waterfall," Rainie said.

"You've got to be kidding."

"If we get up the wall," Rainie said, "it will probably be like any other arroyo."

"Maybe we should go back and try the trail," suggested Denise.

"It looked awful rough to me," Rainie replied. "I was thinking this would be easier for you."

"If I'm going to climb this wall," Denise said as she flipped her long black hair over her shoulders, "I want to know why I'm doing it."

"What do you mean?"

"What do you think is up there?" Denise asked.

"It's not that I know what's up there," Rainie glanced up the twelve-foot wall that rose above them, "but I think I've figured out the petroglyphs."

"I still don't understand."

"You remember the topographic maps that I have been looking at?" Rainie asked.

Denise nodded.

"The contour lines on a topographic map indicate the rise and fall of the land."

"I know that."

"I think the steps on the petroglyphs are like contour lines on a map," Rainie explained, "but the steps indicate levels of the hillside."

"Is that why you had me take a picture of this hill?"

"Yes, there're three levels on the hill above us."

"So you think the Indians or whoever did this petroglyph," Denise pointed at the three-step pyramid, "are saying there is something on top of this hill?"

"You got it," Rainie said. "Hand me your camera."

Denise gave Rainie the camera. Rainie hung it around her neck backwards so the camera rode on her back. She took the canteen off her shoulder and hung it around her neck the same way.

"Ready to climb?" Rainie asked.

Denise nodded.

"Okay," commanded Rainie. "Wedge your right

foot into the crevice and don't close your eyes. It's not that high. I will be right here to help you."

Denise stuck her foot in the crevice and stepped up. "Now what? There's nothing to hold on to."

"Grab the edge of the crevice further up and then step with your left foot up to this knob." Rainie stretched and barely touched the knob with the tips of her fingers.

Denise trembled as she lifted her left foot to the knob. Rainie kept Denise's right foot steady. Now it was up to Denise.

"Can you see any other hand or footholds?"

"I can almost grab the top," Denise said. "Wait. Maybe I can put my right foot on top of this rock."

Rainie looked to the side around Denise's right leg. A rock was wedged in the crevice further up. "Be careful. It might be loose."

Denise slipped her right foot up the crevice and then stepped on the rock. "I can grab the top, but I can't see any more footholds."

"Let me come up behind you and then I'll boost you up." Rainie stepped to where Denise had been and pushed her up.

"Higher," Denise said. "There's nothing to grab onto on top."

Rainie strained and lifted Denise's left foot higher.

"Okay, I think I can make it. Let go." For an instance both of Denise's legs hung over the edge and then somehow she squirmed and pulled herself over the top.

Rainie climbed higher, but she wasn't as tall as Denise. She couldn't grab the top edge. "Are you wearing a belt?" she called.

"No," Denise's voice echoed in the Bath.

Rainie carefully slipped off her belt with her left hand and threw it up and over the edge.

"I've got it," Denise said. She let the end of the belt down.

Rainie grabbed it with her right hand. "Pull," she called.

As Denise pulled, Rainie was able to grasp the top edge with her right hand. Then her left elbow reached the edge. When her right elbow reached the edge, she grasped the belt with both hands and Denise pulled her safely atop the smooth rock.

"Thanks," Rainie puffed.

Denise laid back and put her hands behind her head. "I can't believe we did that," she said.

"It was just a little harder than climbing a bunkbed," Rainie said as she put her belt back on.

"I'm glad you didn't say that down there," Denise exclaimed.

"Why?"

"I fell off my brother's top bunk when I was four. I've always thought that brought on my fear of heights."

"What fear of heights?" Rainie said with a smile as she replaced the canteen on her shoulder. They both chuckled. She handed Denise's camera to her.

"Thanks," Denise said. "I never dreamed that I could do something like that."

"It looks like we might have to walk quite a ways before we can climb out of here," Rainie said. The stone around them was smooth and polished like a giant waterslide, rising to high walls on the sides.

"Look," Denise whispered and pointed. She carefully opened her case and removed her camera.

A rock squirrel perched on a wild grape vine was nibbling on something between its paws. The wild grape vines spilled down into the arroyo like a green waterfall.

Denise snapped one shot of the squirrel from where they stood and then inched closer and took several more shots. Finally, when Denise was no more than ten feet away, the squirrel scrambled back up the vines with annoyed chirps.

"That was great," Denise said. "It was worth the climb."

"Yes," Rainie smiled, "but we'd better try to find a way out of here."

They walked for ten minutes up the arroyo without finding any place that looked promising. Denise stopped once to take a picture of a bunch of miniature barrel cactus in bloom. Rainie thought the cactus looked like castle turrets with red flags flying from them.

They found one place where they could have climbed out, but bunches of prickly pear cactus crowded the narrow gap. Rainie didn't even think a squirrel could crawl through there.

"I think we're going to have to turn back," Rainie said. "We're not getting anywhere."

When they returned to the wall at the Bath, Rainie looked down over the edge. "It looks higher from up here."

Denise stood back from the edge about six feet. "I'm not sure I can go back down it."

"I'll go first," Rainie said. She started to take off her belt.

"But what if I get stuck up here?"

"You won't."

Rainie gave Denise her belt. Denise sat down and Rainie grabbed the belt with both hands. When she backed over the edge, her legs dangled in the air. The slope was pitched inward more than she remembered. She had no way of seeing or feeling the footholds below. For the first time Rainie realized some of the fear that gripped Denise.

"Pull me back up," Rainie said.

They tried three more times, but they were helpless. Neither one was tall enough to reach the first footholds.

"Help!" Denise yelled. "Help!"

Rainie saw the reason Denise was yelling. Mr. McDaniel had just passed on the road below them. Rainie started yelling too, but it was useless. He didn't hear or see them.

"Well, at least we know they found the horses," Denise said. "The guys should be along pretty soon."

"Why didn't he stop?" Rainie asked.

"He probably didn't expect to find the horses this soon and assumed we were still up on the hill."

"This stinks," Rainie said. "I'm sorry I got you into this mess. We should have taken the way you wanted to go."

"That's okay. I've never really done anything like this," Denise said. "It's actually been fun."

"Fun!" Rainie exclaimed. "This is the third time I've got you in trouble."

"That's all right, Rainie. I've been forced to learn more about myself. I've got the feeling now that I can conquer a lot of my fears. I never felt that way about myself before."

Rainie put her head in her hands. She knew that if anyone had helped Denise, God had. She had been so wrapped up in her own desire to solve the petroglyph mystery that she hadn't thought much about anyone else. She half expected a raven to fly over. His cawing would confirm her way of life.

"I'm sorry that I was so bossy the first day when we were climbing," Denise said. "I felt responsible for you. I didn't realize that I was the one who would need to be helped."

"That's okay," Rainie said. "If anyone has a reason to be mad, you do."

They both sat near the edge in quietness. It didn't seem that far down. A large tree grew near the ledge. One branch stretched about six feet from them. If it had been a Robin Hood movie, Robin Hood would have leaped and grabbed the limb and swung down. But they weren't Robin Hood. They were stranded.

"Did you hear that?" Denise said.

Rainie listened. "Someone's coming through the grove."

"Help!" they called. "Help!"

When the boys reached the Bath, Ryan had a mischievous smile across his face. "Inspector Rainie rides again," he said.

"Why'd he say that?" Denise asked.

"Oh, he just likes to make fun of me, especially when he thinks I'm thinking only of solving mysteries." Today Rainie didn't get mad; she knew she deserved it.

"I'll go get my rope," Carl said.

"I guess we should have come with you," Rainie said.

"We didn't need you," Ryan said. "Did you find anything?"

"No, we couldn't find a way to get up the hillside."

"There's a trail back by that boulder," Ryan said.

"We know," Denise replied.

Carl returned with his rope and threw it over the tree limb. "We'll hold the end and you can swing down." Ryan held one end and Carl threw the loop up to Rainie.

"You first, Denise," Carl said. "It'll be just like an elevator. Put one foot in the loop and then swing out."

Denise didn't tremble this time. When she

swung out Ryan and Carl walked toward the slope and slowly let her down.

"Okay, it's time to go," Ryan said. He and Carl turned as if they were going to leave.

"Come on, you guys," Denise pleaded.

Ryan turned back and said, "I guess we'd better let the inspector down."

7

One Step at a Time

After the kids returned the horses, Denise drove Rainie and Ryan the long way home. Aunt Amie was looking out the front window of the ranch house at her birdfeeder when they drove up. Several white-winged doves pecked at feed on the ground below the feeder. They flew off when Ryan slammed the pickup door.

Ryan and Rainie ran in to greet their aunt. She rolled her wheelchair and met them in the hall.

Aunt Amie's welcome smile warmed Rainie all over. She couldn't wait to tell her about the mystery.

"Have you had your lunch?" Aunt Amie asked.

"We're starved," Ryan said.

"There's some leftover steak and potatoes from lunch in the refrigerator."

"I'll warm them up," Rainie said.

While Rainie heated the leftovers in the microwave, Ryan told Aunt Amie about the last three days.

"Where are Uncle Matt and Val and Cinch?" Rainie asked as Ryan dug into his plate.

"They're out working someplace," Aunt Amie said. "I forgot to ask them where they were going after lunch."

"Did they take Ready?" Ryan asked.

"If Ready didn't meet you, he probably went with them," answered Aunt Amie.

Rainie knew Ryan was disappointed. Ready was Uncle Matt's blue heeler. Ryan loved to throw a frisbee to him. They'd never been able to have a dog at home. It was going to be hard for Ryan when they had to go back to Pennsylvania.

Ryan finished his lunch and Rainie saw him go out the back door with a frisbee in his hand.

"What's wrong?" Aunt Amie asked. "You've just been picking at your food."

"I messed up everything when we were out exploring," Rainie said. "If I hadn't been so bullheaded, we might not have been caught in the flood in the first place."

Aunt Amie didn't say anything.

Rainie picked up the plates and glasses, rinsed them, and put them in the dishwasher.

"Did you find out anything about your mystery?" asked Aunt Amie.

The words "your mystery" shook Rainie. She grabbed hold of the counter top and cried.

"What's wrong girl?" Aunt Amie said. "I didn't mean to make you cry." She rolled herself into the kitchen.

Rainie looked down into the sink. "I just messed everything up."

"Ryan didn't say that you'd done anything wrong."

"It's like every way I turned there were roadblocks. Like God was stopping me from solving the mystery."

"Are you sure you weren't stopping yourself?" Aunt Amie asked. "Come sit back down."

Rainie pushed Aunt Amie back to her place at the end of the table and then sat down next to her.

"Maybe you're right," Rainie folded her hands in front of her like she was praying. "Maybe it's me. I've wanted everything to be like it was two weeks ago."

"When you were chasing the lights," Aunt Amie said and smiled.

"Everything seemed to fall into place." Rainie wiped her tears with the backs of her hands. "Now, it's just frustrating. I can't seem to figure out anything."

"Maybe God has something else for you to figure out," Aunt Amie suggested.

"You mean Ryan's mystery."

"Perhaps," Aunt Amie said. "He may have something more important for you to discover than the meaning of the petroglyphs. Maybe He wants to teach you about Himself. Or maybe you'll discover someone who needs your help."

Rainie hadn't thought about it that way. Maybe God did have a different mystery, one that was more important.

"Rainie, most of your unhappiness comes from one thing."

"What?" asked Rainie.

Aunt Amie reached out and placed her left hand on Rainie's right hand. "You've been trying to live the Christian life on your own."

"That's what I thought I was supposed to do." Rainie put her head in her hands and cried.

Rainie felt the warm pressure of Aunt Amie's hand on her arm. She thought about the story of the raven and the dove. Aunt Amie was right. She told Aunt Amie about the raven and the dove and how she felt like she was living like the raven.

"Rainie, God is doing something very special in your life right now. He's trying to teach you how to walk in His Spirit."

Rainie looked up and grabbed a napkin from the napkin holder. She wiped her eyes.

"Let me give you something that may help." Aunt Amie reached with her left hand into the pocket that hung behind her wheelchair. It held her Bible and served like a purse.

"Can I help you?" Rainie asked. She could see that her aunt was fumbling and not finding what she wanted.

"Here it is." Aunt Amie pulled out a green button. "I want you to have this."

Rainie took the button and held it in her palm. It had a brown cross on it with red letters in the cross. They said SAY ES. "I get it; you use the Y twice. It means SAY YES."

Aunt Amie smiled. "Let me explain how you use it. The Y tells what we need to do and the ES tells us how to do it."

"You mean to say yes to Jesus," Rainie said.

"Yes," Aunt Amie said, "but even more than that. Do you know what it means to be filled with the Holy Spirit?"

"No, it has always confused me."

"The Y tells us to yield our rights. The ES tells us how to do it — empty self. We have to empty ourselves before the Lord, so His Spirit can lead us in the way Christ wants us to go."

"Is that why I can't live the Christian life?"

"That's right," Aunt Amie explained. "When we surrender ourselves to the Holy Spirit, the Holy Spirit helps us to live the kind of life Christ wants us to."

"Is that why the Holy Spirit is called the Helper?"

"Yes, He helps us to do for God what we cannot do ourselves."

Rainie rubbed the button between her fingers. "So you're saying that I have been living the Christian life on my own, instead of by the Holy Spirit."

Aunt Amie nodded.

"The Y stands for what?" asked Rainie.

"Yield your rights," answered Aunt Amie.

"The ES?"

"Empty self."

"How do I do that?" asked Rainie.

"You have to be willing to let God live your life."

"I think I'm willing," Rainie said as tears ran down her cheeks. "But what will it mean?"

"You surrender and then take one step at a time in His Spirit. It's a little like learning to understand those petroglyphs you're so interested in. You have to follow the signs," explained Aunt Amie.

"Will I be able to solve the petroglyph mystery?"

"I don't know," Aunt Amie said. "But one thing is certain; when you surrender to the Holy Spirit there is no telling what God can do through you."

"Thank you," Rainie said. "Could you help me?"

Aunt Amie smiled and then they prayed together.

8

Mysterious Smoke

Rainie was pouring birdseed into the feeder in the front yard when Denise drove up the next morning.

"The grader went past an hour ago," Denise said as she leaned out her pickup window. "Do you want to go back to the Bath today?"

Rainie couldn't believe her ears. Why would Denise want to go back after all she had been through? "Just a minute," Rainie said. She poured out the rest of the birdseed. "I'll have to talk to Aunt Amie first."

Rainie rushed into the house and set the birdseed can on the feed sack next to the back door. She heard the clicking of Aunt Amie's computer keyboard in the office.

"Excuse me," she said as she opened the office door.

Aunt Amie turned and smiled.
"You won't believe what just happened. Denise
wants me to go back to the Bath."

"Do you think that's what the Lord would want
you to do?" Aunt Amie rolled her chair backward
and then turned around.

"I'm sure that's what God wants me to do,"
Rainie said excitement filling her voice. "When I
was reading my Bible this morning, I read about
Elijah telling his servant to go back. I wondered
then if maybe God was trying to tell me to return
to the Bath. Now I'm certain. Why would Denise
want to go after all I've put her through?"

"Maybe you'd better go and find out."

"Thanks," Rainie said and she gave her aunt a
hug. Then she turned to leave.

"Wait a minute," Aunt Amie said. "What about
Ryan?"

"What?"

"Remember you told him last night you would
help him with his mystery," reminded Aunt Amie.

Rainie turned back and looked down into her
aunt's brown eyes. Sometimes Rainie felt those
brown eyes would pierce through her. After she
had surrendered her life completely to the Holy
Spirit, she had told Ryan that she would help him
with what he wanted to do.

"Are you saying I can't go?" asked Rainie.

"No, but I don't want you to get caught up in
your mystery if you find something. Ryan is going
to be disappointed that you're gone when he gets

back. What should I tell him?" Aunt Amie asked.

"Tell him that no matter what I find I'm going to help him tomorrow."

"You're sure?" Aunt Amie smiled.

"I'm sure," Rainie said and turned again to leave. "I'll help him no matter how hard it seems."

When Denise and Rainie drove out of the ranch yard, Rainie looked back at the birdfeeder. Two white-winged doves had just landed beneath the feeder. They pecked at the seed Rainie had accidently spilled on the ground.

Rainie felt like laughing; she was so excited. Maybe the doves were a sign. Today, she was going to take her first step in the Spirit.

The path that led up from the Bath was nothing more than a deer trail. Rainie lost it part way up. She led Denise over and around jumbles of rock and brush as they climbed the second level of the hill. She was certain there would be something on top. The hill was shaped just like the petroglyph, two big steps or levels and then the top.

"Wait," Denise called.

Rainie looked back. Denise's pant leg was caught in some cat claw. Cat claw is a low growing viney bush with thorns the shape of cat's claws. Rainie had stepped over it, but Denise was caught.

"Do you need any help?" Rainie asked.

"No, I'm almost free, but I wouldn't mind resting a minute."

Rainie waited in the shade of a large boulder and Denise joined her. "Why did you want to come today?" Rainie asked.

"I've been curious about what might be on top of this hill," Denise said, "because I dreamed we found a great discovery."

"You don't trust dreams, do you?"

"No," Denise said. "I was hoping we might find something neat on top."

"What about your fear of heights?"

"What fear of heights?" Denise smiled. "After what we've been through in the past few days, I'm not worried. If you can do it, I can too."

"You mean this climbing hasn't scared you."

"Well, I'm not exactly comfortable, but I'm not afraid," Denise said. "I guess you could say I'm cautious. That's why I haven't been able to keep up."

"I'll slow down," Rainie said as she stood up. They started up the hill again.

The brush and grass began to thin out the closer they got to the top. Red jagged rocks stuck out of the hillside like spikes on the back of a dinosaur.

Rainie stopped and wiped sweat from her eyes with the back of her hand. For the first time she looked across the valley, instead of looking up. She wasn't sure, but she thought she saw the black rock face below where the Indians etched the five-step pyramid. What about the hillside above the petroglyph? She ought to be able to figure out its levels now.

"What are you looking at?" Denise asked, puffing when she caught up.

"Look at the rim of rocks just above the valley floor. Can you see the dark area between those clusters of rocks?" asked Rainie.

"That's the cliff with the rock art on it."

"That's what I thought," said Rainie. "Now, starting with the cliff and counting it as one, see if you don't count five levels."

"The road is on the third level," Denise said.

"Where the line of juniper trees quits is the fourth level," Rainie added.

"And the long narrow spine of the ridge is the fifth."

"Come on," Rainie said. "I've got an idea." She scrambled up the brow of the hill around a wall of jagged rocks and past a bunch of sotol cactus. The grass grew knee-high on top.

"What is that?" wondered Rainie.

There was an unnatural pile of rocks about four feet tall near the front edge of the hilltop. The hilltop was shaped like a crude triangle, with the top point of the triangle pointing across the valley. The pile of rocks was almost centered at the point of the triangle.

Rainie walked over to the pile of red rocks. It seemed at one time the pile had been higher. Rainie could tell that some of the rocks had fallen off the top. A green moss or lichen grew on one side of the pile.

"I wonder who did that?" Denise asked.

Rainie was so absorbed in her own thoughts she hadn't heard Denise's approach. She looked up, then said, "Probably whoever did the petroglyph."

"But why is it here?" Denise asked.

"I don't know," Rainie said, "but it's kind of disappointing. I don't know what I expected to find, but certainly not just a pile of rocks."

The girls sat silently and gazed across the valley. The ridges across the valley looked like wrinkles on the back of an old man's hand. The San Mateo Mountains rose blue-green in the distance above the wrinkles.

"Could you take some pictures of the rock pile and the levels of the hill across the valley?" Rainie asked. "I think this pile is directly across from the petroglyph."

Denise stood up and opened her camera case. "I think it also lines up with the end of that first narrow ridge," Denise said as she took her camera out of the case.

"I wonder if there are more rock piles on it," Rainie said. "Wait. Look at the second ridge."

"You mean between the second and third ridge?"

"Yeah, it looks like smoke," Rainie said. "Why would anyone be over there?" A thin column of gray rose in the light blue sky.

Denise snapped several pictures and then said, "There hasn't been any rain or lightning in the past few days, so it couldn't be a lightning fire."

"I wonder," Rainie said.

"What?" Denise said as she snapped another picture.

"Aunt Amie said that maybe God had another mystery for us to solve."

"That smoke might have something to do with the plane crash," Denise said.

"Maybe," Rainie said. "But if there had been a fire from the plane crash, the rain last week would have put it out."

"Who or what could it be?"

"I don't know," Rainie said. "But it will be a couple of days before we can check. I've got to help Ryan find Geronimo's gold tomorrow."

"Maybe he'll want to help us solve this," Denise said.

"I doubt it. I think he's got gold fever," Rainie said. She stood up. "We'd better get back."

9

Ryan's Way

Rainie was right. Ryan had gold fever. He wasn't impressed by the smoke or the rock pile. So now they were doing everything his way, much to Cinch's dissatisfaction. Cinch was one of Uncle Matt's ranch hands. His tanned face was wrinkled like the mountainside, his legs were bowed from decades on horseback, and his disposition was like a grizzly bear. Somehow Ryan had convinced Uncle Matt that he needed Cinch's help.

Since early morning they had been riding up San Mateo Canyon. Ryan was sure he could find some clue that would lead them to Geronimo's gold. Cinch had complained all the way.

The horses' hooves made little clouds of dust as they rode up the road. It was hard to believe that they already needed rain again. Ryan and Carl led out, Rainie followed, and Cinch complained about riding drag—being last.

"When are we going to turn back, Ranger?" Cinch yelled.

All day Cinch had called Ryan, Ranger. Rainie guessed he was referring to the Lone Ranger. Ryan ignored Cinch and kept riding. Rainie turned in her saddle and looked back at Cinch. He wiped his wrinkled face and waterfall mustache with a bandanna and then put it back in his pocket.

"Hey Ranger," he yelled. "Could we at least trade places so I don't have to eat your dust anymore?"

Ryan just ignored him.

Rainie had to admit that she was tired, too. She didn't know what Ryan expected to find. Besides that she felt out of place. Denise couldn't come because she had to go to town with her mom. Rainie hadn't realized till now how close she and Denise had become as friends. She missed her.

Rainie wondered where this day was going to lead. It seemed wasted so far. At least Denise had taken her film to town to get it developed. Maybe they could figure out something when the pictures came back.

Rainie had committed the day to the Lord that morning. Now she prayed again and asked God to teach her and use her even if it was just honoring a promise to her brother.

"Look's like somebody's got car trouble," Carl said.

Rainie stood up in the stirrups and looked ahead over Carl's shoulder. A battered brown truck blocked the road.

As they approached the truck a large yellow dog ran out wagging its tail. It panted and panted. Rainie thought he might lick them to death.

A man with a red bandanna over his head and a long ponytail yelled at the dog, "Gold! Get back." The dog trotted back toward the man with its tail between its legs. The man got a short length of rope and tied the dog to a bush.

"Need some help?" Ryan called out.

"No, I'm almost finished," he turned and said.

At that moment when he turned, Rainie thought the man looked somehow familiar. Was it the blonde hair and beard? The muscular build? The sunglasses?

The man bent down and hand-tightened a lug nut as though to ignore them.

They all got off their horses and gathered around where the man was working.

Cinch cleared his throat and said, "Stranger, you know this is private land."

"I know," he said without looking up from his work. "I was trying to get on the national forest. I must have picked up a mesquite thorn back down the road a ways."

"Do you have permission to be on this land?" Cinch persisted.

The stranger stood for the first time. He towered over Cinch. He looked like a giant pirate because of the way he wore his red bandanna. "I don't need permission. This is a public road," he said. He jerked the bandanna further down on his forehead.

Rainie stepped forward and extended her hand, "I'm sorry. We didn't introduce ourselves. I'm Rainie Trevors and this is my brother Ryan. And these are our friends Carl and Cinch."

The man's hand swallowed Rainie's, but he didn't say a thing. He turned back to his work and put on the last lug nut.

"What's yours?" Rainie asked.

"People call me Demas." He began tightening the nuts with the lug wrench.

Rainie thought Demas's powerful biceps would pop the short sleeves of his T-shirt as he turned the wrench. The lug nuts squeaked as he finished tightening each one.

"Don't you think your dog needs a drink?" Ryan asked.

The dog looked miserable panting in the shade of a bush where Demas had tied him.

"Gold will get a drink when I get one."

"What are you doing up here?" Cinch asked.

"Looking for lost kids," Demas said through a crooked tooth smile. "Why are you up here?"

"I guess you could say we're treasure hunting," Rainie said.

"You'd shouldn't have told him that," Ryan whispered in her ear.

The smile disappeared from Demas's face. "You

might as well turn back. There's no treasure up here." He inserted the lug wrench in the jack and lowered the truck.

"We have permission to be up here," Cinch said.

Demas stood up and glared down at Cinch with the lug wrench in his hand.

Rainie thought Demas was going to hit Cinch.

Ryan pulled on Cinch's arm, "We'd better turn back if we're going to get home before dark."

"Let's be neighborly and help the man first," Cinch said. He grabbed the flattened tire and took it around the back of the truck and threw it up on the tailgate.

Demas threw the jack and lug wrench in back. "I don't need your help," he hissed.

Rainie noticed a long narrow piece of white metal sticking out from under a canvas. Quickly Demas pulled the canvas over it, closed the tailgate and the topper door. Then he walked around the other side of the battered truck to avoid them. He untied the dog and put him in the truck cab. The engine started and they were showered with dust as he drove away.

"Nice man," Carl said.

"I wouldn't want to meet him in a dark alley," Ryan added. "We'd better get back."

"It's about time, Ranger," Cinch said as he turned his horse back down the road.

"Did you notice something familiar about him?" Rainie asked.

"What are you talking about?" Ryan said as he

mounted his horse.

Rainie mounted and rode up beside him. "I thought something was familiar about him when I first saw him. I didn't notice what it was until I thought he was going to hit Cinch."

"What did you notice?" Ryan asked.

"He was wearing my sunglasses," Rainie said, "the ones I lost when we found the airplane wheel."

"Are you sure?" Ryan asked.

"Where would he get sunglasses exactly like mine?"

"You mean Uncle Matt's."

Rainie ignored his tease. "Demas must have been above the petroglyph if he found my sunglasses. I wonder why he was up there."

"Inspector Rainie rides again," Ryan teased and then rode ahead to join the others.

Rainie rode drag now, but she didn't mind. It gave her time to think. She felt excited again. Maybe Aunt Amie was right. Maybe God had another mystery for her to solve. Rainie thanked the Lord that she had come today. She felt sure she had taken another step in the Spirit.

10

The Sign of the Doves

The next day Denise and Rainie climbed the hill above the five-step petroglyph. Thunderheads rose like a great snowy mountain range above the Black Range Mountains to the southwest.

"We're going to have to get back down before too long," Denise said. "Those clouds look like they could cause us some trouble."

"You're right. I sure don't want to get stuck again. I'm sorry we couldn't get an earlier start," Rainie said. "Aunt Amie needed my help."

"Won't Ryan be mad that you didn't wait for him?" asked Denise.

"No, he talked Val into trying to teach him to rope this afternoon. He wants to learn to rope like Carl," answered Rainie.

Rainie walked up one track of the two-track road

and Denise walked beside her in the other.

"What are we looking for?" Denise asked.

"The tracks of Demas's truck. I wonder if I lost my sunglasses when I crossed this road."

"You know he was up here if he found your glasses."

"I know," Rainie took her cap off and wiped her forehead with the back of her hand. "I was hoping to find some clue as to why he was up here."

"He must have been looking for something," suggested Denise.

"But what?"

When they finally found the tire tracks, the tracks turned off the road and went out to the flat area where the helicopter had landed. Denise and Rainie followed where the truck had smashed down the grass.

"I think he must have seen the helicopter land," Rainie said. "Why else would he have come up here?"

"That would mean he might have been watching us," Denise said.

"Wow," Rainie said and grabbed her head with both hands. "What have I been thinking?"

Denise looked puzzled.

Rainie pointed at the tracks. "These were made after the rain. He's probably been up here twice."

"When he saw us and when he came after the rain," Denise added.

"But why?" Rainie said. "We'd better check if there's anything on the top of this hill."

As they climbed the hill, they discussed various reasons why Demas would have been up there. "He could be a drug smuggler," Denise said.

"I've never seen a drug smuggler," Rainie said, "but he doesn't strike me as one."

"What if he saw the plane go down?"

"No, what if he found other parts of the plane," Rainie said, "like what I saw in his truck?"

"Are you sure you're not imagining things?" Denise asked.

"I'll know tomorrow," Rainie said. "After church I'm going to see if Uncle Matt will drop me by the airport. If I can get a good look at a small plane maybe I can figure it out."

"You could also pick up my film while you're in town," said Denise.

"I'd be glad to," Rainie said.

They walked on in silence. Rainie pondered all the possibilities Demas had for being here yesterday. Maybe he could be a drug smuggler. But then, when she mentioned treasure hunting he changed the subject or at least tried to discourage them. Maybe he was looking for Geronimo's gold. Maybe that was why his dog was named Gold.

Rainie and Denise were both puffing when they reached the spine of the ridge. And they still had to climb the ridge to the top.

Denise pointed to a column of smoke only one ridge away. But it still seemed a long way off. "That looks like the same place we saw smoke the other day."

"Who could it be?" Rainie said. "Why would they need to build a fire this time of day?"

"They could be signaling for help," Denise suggested.

"Maybe."

Denise and Rainie started up the ridge. "We'd better hurry," Rainie said. "Look at the clouds." The line of clouds still hung dark and threatening.

Now they were on the edge of the foothills. "We can't turn back now," Denise said.

"Look." Rainie pointed at a pile of rocks in the distance.

"You were right," Denise smiled and said.

Somehow Rainie didn't feel too excited. Now she had something to tell the archaeologist, but what?

There were seven rock piles in a line on this ridge. All directly across from the other rock pile on the opposite hillside. But from this distance you couldn't see the rock pile. She had obviously figured out the petroglyphs. They were like traffic signs directing those ancient people to the tops of these hills. But why?

Did the people carry rocks up to the tops of these hills in some strange ritual? Could the rock piles be graves? Or could something else be hidden under them?

Denise busied herself taking pictures of the rock piles from different angles.

Rainie turned her attention from the rock piles to the smoke column. Could somebody be calling for help?

She knew she should feel excited, but somehow she felt troubled in her spirit. Solving mysteries wasn't a game anymore. What if someone really needed help?

"I'm done," Denise said. "It looks like we're going to be all right. The clouds are breaking up."

Rainie glanced up at the sky. The clouds drifted by like tattered rags. If it rained it probably wouldn't be any big storm.

On the way back down to Denise's truck, Rainie heard the cooing of doves twice. She felt like God was giving her signs. She knew she was walking in the Spirit. But why did she feel troubled? She'd have to talk to Aunt Amie. God obviously had another mystery for her to solve, but this time she felt it wasn't a game. What could it be? It was all so confusing. She'd have to make sure she took one step at a time in the Spirit. She was thankful God had given her the sign of the doves.

11

Burdened

Rainie and Aunt Amie visited in the backseat while Uncle Matt, Val and Ryan talked about sports in the front as they drove to church the next morning. For the first time since she'd come to New Mexico, Rainie felt like Aunt Amie didn't understand her problem.

"Sometimes God uses His word to lead us, sometimes He uses people, but at other times He uses circumstances," Aunt Amie said.

Rainie still felt confused and very tired. She had run all over the hills in her mind last night and slept fitfully.

Why should she be so bothered? She was certain she had been surrendering her will and life to God. The petroglyph mystery was now almost solved and she had something to share with the archaeologist. But why were the rock piles on the hills? Why was there smoke on the next ridge over? And why had Demas been above the petroglyph?

The smoke was the problem. Something about it almost called out to her. She had talked to Uncle Matt and then called and talked to Mr. McDaniel. Both of them agreed that there shouldn't be anyone up there, and they both said that if it had been a lightning fire it would have burned out or spread by now.

Who was it? Who kept building the fire? What if it was some sort of signal?

Rainie enjoyed her Sunday school class, but just like the smoke on the ridge, her mind kept drifting away during the lesson. It bothered her, because she usually had no problem paying attention.

Rainie pushed Aunt Amie up the aisle before the morning worship service. She had never seen a church so packed with people.

"Right here will be fine," Aunt Amie said.

Rainie pushed Aunt Amie as close to the edge of the pew as she could, then sat down next to her aunt. Uncle Matt and Ryan helped some other men put out more chairs.

"Why don't you go sit with the young people?" Aunt Amie suggested.

"I just want to sit next to you," said Rainie.

"Is something wrong?" Aunt Amie reached out and touched Rainie's arm.

"I'm just so confused."

She didn't have a chance to say more because it

was time for the service to start. Uncle Matt sat down next to Rainie. Ryan sat down front with some of the other kids.

When the singing started, Rainie forgot her problems. The songs helped her focus on the Lord instead of her dilemma. The words of the songs created an expectancy that God was going to move in a special way during the service.

Val played guitar with another man and helped lead the song service. To Rainie, Val always seemed to be smiling, but even more so now. She wondered if angels smiled like he did; his whole face gleamed with joy.

Rainie looked back down at the hymnal she was sharing with Uncle Matt and then turned and smiled at Aunt Amie. Aunt Amie winked at her.

During Pastor Walker's message, one thought excited Rainie. Pastor Walker said, "Sometimes God places a burden on our hearts just as He did in the life of Jesus and in Paul's life. We have a sense that we have to do something for God. Paul felt a burden to go to Jerusalem and so did our Lord. Maybe God has placed a burden on your heart. Don't turn away. No matter how heavy it may seem, obey Him."

Now Rainie knew. God had placed a burden on her heart. A burden to solve His mystery, not hers. She couldn't wait to find out about the smoke. God had led Israel with a column of smoke and fire, hadn't He? Maybe that was the way He was going to lead her.

After the service, they picked up Denise's pictures and then went out to lunch.

"I can't believe all that you and Denise have done," Uncle Matt said after lunch. He had the pictures spread out between Aunt Amie and himself. He held up one of the pictures. "I'd say this is more than just a campfire."

"But who could be up there?" Aunt Amie asked.

"That's what I'd like to know!" Rainie exclaimed.

"Is it all right if I help her tomorrow?" Ryan asked Uncle Matt.

"But it's my turn to help you with your mystery," Rainie interrupted.

"I don't care whose mystery you solve," Uncle Matt said. "Val and Cinch will have to help me tomorrow."

After lunch they drove out to the city airport and the attendant let Ryan and Rainie look at some of the small planes. Rainie pointed at a long narrow piece of metal that connected one of the plane's wheels. "I think this piece is what was in the back of Demas's truck," she said.

"That's a strut," the attendant said.

Then Rainie remembered the helicopter. She took the photos out of her purse and flipped through the pictures of the helicopter. "Have you ever seen a black helicopter like this flying around here?"

"Sure," the attendant said. "A while back, we had a plane crash here. And almost before anyone else could get to the wreckage a black unmarked helicopter landed and took over the investigation."

"Who or what was it?" Rainie asked.

"The DEA."

"The who?" Rainie asked.

"The United States Drug Enforcement Agency."

"Whoa," Rainie said. Then she thought about the radio. She would have to get it back from Mr. McDaniel and see if she could return it to the drug agent who lost it.

As Ryan and Rainie walked back to the car Ryan asked, "What are you going to do?"

"Get the radio back first and then find out who's making that smoke," replied Rainie.

12

Mysterious Signs

"You see this button?" Mr. McDaniel showed the radio to Rainie. "You hold it down when you want to speak."

"Do you really think we should take it with us?" Rainie asked.

"It would be better for you to take it and use it if you need help than for it to just sit here," Mr. McDaniel said. "Besides that, I found out that the DEA is based out of El Paso. It may be a while before we can take the radio down there."

"And maybe we'll run across them again," Ryan said.

Rainie didn't know if she liked that thought, but she took the radio and packed it in the saddle bags. Then she mounted her horse. Ryan, Rainie, Denise and Carl turned and waved back to Mr. McDaniel as they rode out of the yard.

They rode west up Monticello Canyon past the five-step petroglyph and then turned north up Shipman Canyon. Mr. McDaniel had said that the canyon would be the easiest way to find out where the smoke was coming from. Shipman Canyon ran down from the San Mateo Mountains and wound down like a snake to Monticello Canyon. It was obvious by the debris hanging in the brush and on the sides of the canyon that it had run a lot of water during the last flood.

"Do you think those clouds are going to be any problem?" Rainie asked Denise.

"No," Denise said. "They're past us. It may be raining up in the San Mateos, but we should be okay."

"I don't see any smoke," Ryan said as he pulled his horse next to Rainie's.

"We were up above both times when we saw it," Rainie said, "and I don't think we could see it from down here, because of the height of the canyon walls."

Denise looked up. "I don't think there's any place that we could ride up to get on top if we wanted to."

"Mr. McDaniel said we probably have to leave the horses and climb," stated Rainie.

"Great," Denise said and smiled at Rainie.

"I've got my rope," Carl said.

"I've got mine, too," Ryan yelled.

"That's comforting," Denise said.

Rainie and Denise smiled at each other and let

the guys take the lead. Ryan and Carl were going to be surprised at how good Denise had become in her climbing.

They had ridden for about five minutes when Rainie pointed above them and asked Denise, "Don't you think that's the ridge with the rock piles?"

"I'm sure it is," Denise said. "If we keep riding we should be able to find a side arroyo that we can climb."

"When we see the top of the next ridge, we'll be almost there," Rainie said.

"Hey, we found something," Ryan yelled.

Carl and Ryan galloped back toward them. Ryan had a gray board in his hand with something red on it.

"Look," Ryan held the board out to Rainie. "Someone has scratched 'help' on it."

"I think this is a girl's or woman's hairband," Rainie said as she fingered the red thing.

"Where'd you find it?" Denise asked.

"It was stuck in a bush," Ryan said. "I saw the red and wondered what it was."

"I don't see anyone around here that needs help," Rainie said as she glanced over her shoulder. "This is a mysterious sign," remarked Rainie. "I wonder . . . do you think it was washed down in the big flood?"

"Then it's been lying here a while," said Carl. "That was over a week ago."

"The same time as the plane crash," Ryan said.

"I've got a feeling this doesn't have anything to do with the plane," Rainie said.

Denise and Rainie looked at each other and almost said at the same time . . . "The smoke!"

"Someone has been trying to call for help," Denise said.

"Someone probably threw this sign in a small arroyo on top and it has washed all the way down here," exclaimed Rainie.

"I bet it's a girl or woman that needs help because the person probably took off her hairband and put it on this board as another sort of sign to catch our attention," said Denise.

"We'd better try to get up there," Ryan said and he took the lead again. "We'd better do it fast."

Rainie looked at the weathered board a little longer, then reached back and put it in her saddlebags. Now she knew why God had placed the burden on her heart. These mysterious signs meant someone was in trouble. She kicked her horse with her heels and tried to catch up with the others.

When she had almost caught them she heard Carl yell, "Turn back!"

"Flood!" Ryan yelled as he and Carl passed her.

Rainie turned her horse and almost ran into Denise. They followed Carl and Ryan at a fast gallop up a little finger of land that stuck out from the side of the canyon. The finger rose about eight feet above the canyon floor.

They heard the water first, its volume magnified

in the narrow confines of the canyon. Then, in less than a minute, a four or five foot wall of water rushed by them. Muddy water slapped against the thumb and splashed at the horses' hooves.

Rainie took a deep breath; she didn't realize she had been holding her breath. That was a close escape. Now what would they do? How would they find out who made the mysterious sign? How would they ever help whoever was trapped?

13

Followed

"**I**'m sorry," Denise said as they rode back to the McDaniel Ranch. "I never dreamed that it was raining that much up in the San Mateos."

"That's okay," Rainie said. "I'm just glad we had that little piece of high ground. Otherwise we might have been in real trouble."

They'd had to wait two hours for the water to recede before they could start back. Rainie thanked the Lord again and again for Carl's sharp hearing and for the little rise of land.

Then she thought about the board. If they hadn't found it then, they might never have found it. Who knows where the flood would have washed it. She thanked the Lord for His timing and direction and then asked Him to help whoever was in trouble. *Please help them to hold on until we can get to them.*

Early the next morning they headed back up Shipman Canyon. Not a single cloud sailed in the sky. So far the weatherman was right. It was supposed to be clear across the whole state. But that's what the weatherman had predicted the day before.

Rainie was grateful that they'd brought the radio. They almost needed it yesterday. She also felt grateful because Uncle Matt and Cinch were around if she needed more help. They and several other ranchers were helping Mr. McDaniel rebuild his corrals today.

But she was also puzzled. Late yesterday afternoon, Mr. McDaniel had called a friend who owned a plane at the airport. He described the area where they had seen the smoke and asked the pilot to fly over it. When he flew over, he saw nothing, no sign of anything unusual. Mr. McDaniel had also called the sheriff about the board and hairband. But the sheriff said he'd check it out and get back to him.

What was going on, Rainie wondered. They had all been so excited after finding the board, but now she'd had to talk Ryan into coming along. He wanted to stay and help the men build the corrals. Even Denise had been skeptical about going back. "There's no telling how long that board's been there," she said.

They rode silently. The only sounds were the horses' shoes scraping in the gravel.

"I think that's about where I found the board yesterday," Ryan said as they passed a bunch of bent over bushes.

"We were almost there yesterday," Denise said and pointed. The second ridge rose above them.

"It's not as steep as the one above the Bath," Rainie said.

"We could climb that," Ryan said, but the sound of his voice wasn't very enthusiastic.

"Let's find an arroyo farther on," Rainie suggested.

About a hundred yards down the canyon, they found a sharp gap where an arroyo had cut between the ridges. "That should lead where we need to go," Denise said.

They rode across the canyon and picketed their horses on a small bench a safe distance above the canyon floor and then walked back to the arroyo.

"Wait," Rainie said. "Let's pray first. I want to make sure we start out right."

Rainie prayed for God's protection and leading. Before she was finished praying she heard the cooing of a dove above them. "Thank you, Lord. Amen," she said louder than necessary.

"What was that about?" Ryan said. "You sounded like a preacher."

"Oh, it's sort of a long story," Rainie said. "You may not understand. But I think of that dove as a sign from the Lord that I'm following His leading."

Ryan and Carl took the lead again and Rainie hung back with Denise in case she needed help. Rainie started up after Denise but then she remembered the radio and the canteen.

"Go ahead," she said to Denise. "I'll catch up."

She ran back to the horses and got the radio and canteen. She hung the canteen over her shoulder and turned to look up. Ryan, Carl and Denise were already quite a ways up the arroyo. Denise was right with the guys. Rainie stuffed the radio in the waistband of her jeans and started after them.

She scrambled up the arroyo moving as fast as she safely could, but she couldn't hear or see the others above. Climbing from polished boulder to boulder, she grabbed brush or rocks wherever she could find handholds. After she'd climbed five or ten minutes, she began to worry. It seemed like she had climbed hundreds of stairs. Certainly they would have needed a rest by now.

The arroyo started to level out; it was more like a gradual slide than stairs now. She knew it would still be a while before she got to its head. She stopped and wiped the sweat from her eyes with the back of her hand. Then called, "Ryan, wait up."

Her voice echoed back down the canyon. From up above she heard a distant, "We're up here."

She sighed and thanked the Lord. Then she stepped out again. But she felt strange. Once in a while she heard noises behind her, like scraping or dragging. She stopped. There it was again. A definite scrape. It could be one of Ryan's jokes. Maybe they had doubled back and were following her.

She ran ahead and hid in the shade of a boulder where she would be able to see their approach. The scraping and dragging sound kept coming toward her. She wondered if it was wise to wait for it. Maybe she shouldn't.

From her crouch beside the boulder, she saw the animal's head first. It was a dog, or what looked like a dog. It pulled with its front legs and dragged its hind legs. Something was really wrong with it. One eye was swollen shut and there was dried blood on its head and back. It couldn't even see Rainie.

She didn't know what to do. Injured animals weren't anything to mess with.

Wait. She recognized it. It was Demas's dog. What would it be doing up here?

"Come here, Gold," she called. The dog turned its head toward her. She edged closer toward it. What should she do now?

She could see that the dog's left eye was okay. "Come here, Gold." She stretched out her up-turned palm. He laid his head on her hand and let out a weak whine.

"Good boy, Gold. We'll help you out." Rainie rubbed him behind his head. What had happened to him?

"Ryan, come back," she yelled. "Ryan, come back."

This dog needed help now. She couldn't wait for the others. She thought of the canteen. Rainie took it off her shoulder and poured a little water in her hand. Gold lapped the water eagerly.

"Ryan, come back," she yelled louder this time. "I need your help."

"We're coming," she heard echo from above.

She poured more water in her hand and let the dog drink.

"What do you need?" Ryan yelled from above.

"Come take a look," Rainie yelled back.

She heard the slap of their running feet against stone and gravel before she saw them.

"This better be good," Ryan said, puffing as he approached.

Rainie stroked the uninjured side of Gold's head.

"That's Demas's dog!" Ryan exclaimed.

"No kidding," Rainie said. "I don't know how we passed him by, because he started following me. I thought you guys were playing a joke on me when I heard him dragging himself along."

Denise knelt down and started examining him. "I think someone has beat him. Look at these welts." She pointed at the brown ugly stripes across his head and back.

"I wonder what he's doing up here?" Ryan asked.

"Maybe he saw us pass yesterday." Carl pointed below. "I think that's where we found the board."

"That makes sense," Ryan said, "but how did we pass him today?"

"I think he was probably hidden," Rainie said. "He wouldn't be able to defend himself from predators. And he couldn't drag himself out of hiding fast enough when he heard us pass."

"What are we going to do with him?" Denise asked.

"Wait," Carl said. "Listen."

Ryan tried to say something, but Carl held his finger to his lips.

Then they heard it. Someone was yelling for help above.

14

The Rescue

The yelling stopped.

"I'll stay with the dog," Denise offered. "You better see who it is."

The boys ran back up the arroyo.

"Are you sure?" Rainie asked.

"Get going," Denise said and smiled.

"Wait up, guys," Rainie yelled as she ran to catch up.

The voice called out again.

"We're coming!" Ryan yelled.

Rainie slipped and almost fell. She decided to slow down. I won't be able to help anyone if I don't settle down, she thought.

Ryan kept yelling, "We're coming!"

Rainie saw the boys scramble up the arroyo bank as they followed the sound of the voice.

Now the voice yelled, "Get me out!"

Rainie heard pounding as she climbed up the bank out of the arroyo. When she reached the boys, they were trying to kick in the door of a cabin.

A hand stuck out of a hole where a stove pipe had been pushed out. The hand waved and the voice begged, "Please get me out."

Rainie was sure it was a girl; she sounded almost hysterical.

"Quit, Ryan," Rainie yelled. "You can't get her out that way. Look at those bolts." Two bolts had been pushed through two hasps and then fastened with nuts.

Ryan kept pounding on the door.

"Get me out." The voice sounded desperate.

"Settle down, Ryan," Rainie said. "We'll get her out."

Ryan finally quit pounding.

Rainie tried to reassure the person, "Don't worry. We're here. We'll get you out. Just give us a minute to undo these bolts."

Carl knelt and unfastened the bottom nut and removed the bolt. Rainie unfastened the top nut and bolt. The door swung inward.

The girl ran into Rainie's arms. "Thank you, thank you," she sobbed. She rubbed her eyes and blinked, trying to adjust to the bright light. Her clothes were black with soot, her blonde hair matted, and her face gray with soot. She smelled like a chimney.

"Water. Do you have any water?" she asked. "I

haven't had anything to drink in two days."

Rainie patted her side feeling for the canteen. She'd left it with Denise. "Ryan, run back and get the water. Carl, see if you can help Denise get that dog up here."

"What dog?" the girl asked.

"It's a miner's dog named Gold," Rainie answered.

"I haven't seen them in four days," responded the girl.

"Who?" Rainie asked.

"Demas and Gold," she said. "He kidnapped me."

"He kidnapped you!" Ryan exclaimed.

The girl began to sob. Rainie noticed that she was also shivering.

Rainie gently put her hand on the girl's shoulder. "Come on," she said. "Let's go sit in the sun."

"Ryan, go get the water," commanded Rainie.

Ryan turned and left. Carl followed.

"What's your name?" asked Rainie.

"Andrea Brendan."

"I'm Rainie. How long have you been up here?"

"Two months, I think. He thinks I'm his daughter. He kidnapped me the last week of school."

"Why'd he think you were his daughter?"

"His ex-wife took his daughter after their divorce and disappeared. He was visiting Albuquerque and drove past where I went to school. I guess I look just like his daughter and I'm the same age.

He calls me Angela. I had to call him Dad."

"What have you done all this time?" asked Rainie.

"He'd let me out to gather firewood. That's when I scratched help on a board and threw it in the arroyo. Did you find it?"

"We sure did." Rainie took a minute to study the cabin. It was built under a rock overhang and its rockwork almost blended into the overhang. It must have been like a dungeon.

"I'm so thirsty and hungry." Andrea swept her hair out of her face and tucked it behind her ears. "I must look terrible."

"It doesn't matter," Rainie said. "I'm sure there are going to be a lot of people very pleased to know you're alive."

Andrea started to cry again.

Rainie heard rocks sliding in the arroyo. Ryan came over the top with the canteen. He handed it to Rainie. She unscrewed the cap and passed the water to Andrea. "You'd better just drink a little at a time. It might make you sick," she said.

Andrea drank a little, then poured some water on her hands and wet her face. "Thank you," she said. She smiled for the first time since she'd been rescued.

Rainie stood up as she heard Carl and Denise coming up the arroyo bank. Denise struggled up the bank with Gold. She laid the dog next to Andrea.

"Gold," Andrea reached out and stroked his

head. "Who did this to you?"

"Probably Demas," Ryan said.

"Not Demas," Andrea said. "He never hit him."

"Then what happened?" demanded Ryan.

"I don't know." Andrea took another drink. "Just before he left the last time, Demas said we were going to be rich soon."

"How was he going to get rich?" Rainie asked.

"He was looking for Geronimo's gold mine, but I don't think he found it. He would've said so," answered Andrea.

"What are we going to do?" Denise said.

"I think San Mateo Canyon is only about a mile from here," Carl said. "One of us could go get the horses and ride back to the ranch."

"That's a great idea," Rainie said. "Then we could walk out to the road in San Mateo Canyon."

"Why don't Carl and I go," suggested Ryan.

"What are we going to do with Gold?" Andrea asked.

"We could make a stretcher," Carl said. "It would probably be easier to carry him out to the road, than back down the arroyo."

"We'll make it before we go," Ryan said.

Ryan and Carl disappeared inside the cabin. In a few seconds, Ryan reappeared in the doorway. "There's nothing in here."

"I'm sorry," Andrea said. "I burned everything. When Demas didn't come back I thought it was my only hope."

"That's why we saw smoke the past two days. It

was you. And you really did need help," exclaimed Rainie. "I felt such a burden when I saw that smoke, but I didn't know exactly why. I thought it was some sort of sign."

Rainie fell silent for a moment. Wow, she thought, I really was following the leading of the Holy Spirit. How terrible it would have been for Andrea if I hadn't obeyed His Spirit and investigated the smoke.

"Well, we can use our T-shirts to make a stretcher," Carl said.

"You won't have to do that," Andrea went into the cabin and reappeared with a rumpled sleeping bag. "Here. Use this." She held it at arm's length as though something was wrong with it.

"Phew," Ryan said when he grabbed it. "It smells like a burnt log."

Carl and Ryan made the stretcher while the girls discussed their plans.

"Do you think you can walk out?" Denise asked Andrea.

"I'll be fine. Just let me have another drink. I can't wait to get home. I'm sure my folks are dying with worry."

Ryan and Carl lifted Gold carefully onto the stretcher. He seemed to sense that they would take care of him.

"Tell Uncle Matt we'll be waiting at the road for you," said Rainie.

The boys turned to go.

"Wait," Rainie said.

Ryan smiled, "I know. We forgot to pray." This time Ryan led them in prayer and then they parted to go their separate ways.

15

Vultures

The girls descended from the ridge following the tracks where Demas's truck had passed. The landscape was spotted with junipers and pinons. Below them San Mateo Canyon stretched its way toward the San Mateo Mountains. They could see the gradual landscape change from the grassy mesa tops, to the juniper spotted hills, and finally to the pine covered slopes of the mountains.

"Did you ever get to see this view?" Rainie asked Andrea.

"No, it was nighttime when he brought me here."

"I think it's beautiful," said Rainie.

Denise led carrying the front of the stretcher and Rainie held the back. Andrea followed them as they made their way slowly out onto the road.

"Look over there," said Denise, "looks like a
feast." Ahead of them the canyon forked like a
snake's tongue. Where the canyon forked a side-
canyon entered the main one. The road ran down
the canyon and disappeared up the right fork.
Midway up the left fork a group of ten or fifteen
vultures circled. They hovered over the tall pines
that grew out of the canyon floor.

"I wonder what died?" Rainie said.

"I don't think it's dead yet," Denise replied.

"I'm surprised they're not circling over us,"
Andrea said. "Gold doesn't look too good."

"I think he'll make it," Denise said.

When they reached the road, they rested in the
shade. But Rainie was troubled. "I keep thinking
about those vultures," Rainie said. Something
about their presence made her feel worried.

"Don't tell me," Denise said, "you want to go
check."

"Don't you think the guys would be reaching the
horses about now?" Rainie asked.

"We had a little farther to walk and we had the
stretcher," Denise said.

"Even if they have reached the horses," Rainie
said, "they still have to ride back to the McDaniel's
and then they have to drive the long way around
to get back up here. We could check out what's up
there and be back to the road before they pass.
And to make sure they don't miss us, we could
leave rock arrows in the road so they know which
way we've gone."

"We don't have much water left," Denise said.

"How are you doing?" Rainie asked Andrea.

"I'm fine," she answered as she rubbed Gold behind his uninjured eye. "But what about him?"

"We'll have to take him," Rainie said. "Our walking on the road won't hurt him anymore than the ride out of here."

"If we take it slow," Denise said, "we should be okay."

Rainie and Denise gathered rocks and made an arrow pointing up the road. About every two hundred yards, they stopped and let Andrea rest. Then they gathered more stones and made more arrows.

When they reached the side canyon the road continued up the main canyon. They made an arrow pointing up the side canyon.

Thick brush lined the edge of the road where the side canyon entered San Mateo. When Rainie parted a bush to try and make her way through, the bush came loose in her hand.

"Someone has driven through here," Rainie said.

Rainie and Denise picked up Gold again and they followed the path where a vehicle had smashed down the grass and brush. The canyon turned sharply and then straightened out again. Huge pine trees blocked much of the sunlight from reaching the canyon floor. They traveled slowly.

"There's something blocking the way ahead," Denise said.

It looked like a wall of brush again, but then Rainie caught sight of a strange reflection.

"Let's put Gold down," Rainie said.

They set the stretcher down and then Rainie ran ahead. She swept cut branches to the side, exposing the back of a truck.

"Hey, this is Demas's. I wonder where he is?" Andrea stuttered. "Maybe we should turn back."

"Look," Denise said. "All the tires have been slashed."

"Someone hid the trail and truck so it couldn't be seen. I wonder what happened to Demas," Rainie said. "It seems as though he has some enemies. Do you think the same person who did this could be the one who hurt Gold?"

"If they did, then maybe they hurt Demas, too," said Denise.

"I wonder if he's still alive," said Rainie. The girls went back and picked up the stretcher.

"Are you thinking what I'm thinking?" Rainie asked Denise.

"Yes," Denise said. "I think Demas found more than he bargained for."

"Is it safe to go on?" Andrea asked.

As they walked back past the truck Rainie said, "Whoever did this has been gone for awhile. I don't think we have anything to worry about."

Then Rainie heard the caw of a raven ahead. *Lord,* she prayed silently, *I'm not seeking my own way but Yours. Please help us.*

"Is something wrong?" Denise asked.

"No, I think everything is going to be all right." Rainie paused. She realized the burden she had felt during the last several days was gone. *Thank You, Lord. No matter what lies ahead, I know that You have been leading me just as You led us to Andrea.*

An island of sunlight pierced through the forest canopy ahead. They could see that something had broken through the trees. Vultures hovered over the island of light.

The path was again hidden by brush, but this time white patches of something shone through. The girls quickly pushed aside the cut branches. There in front of them lay a crashed white plane.

"I knew it," Rainie said, "back there when we found the truck."

Andrea walked around the plane pulling brush off it.

"I can't believe we found it," Denise said.

"We didn't find it," Rainie said. "God led us."

Denise looked at Rainie with a puzzled expression.

"I'll explain it all to you later," Rainie said. "I've just been learning to follow His leading." She took a deep breath. "I just wish Ryan were here. He's going to be disappointed."

"Hey, over here," Andrea called, "It's Demas."

They hadn't even noticed that they still held the stretcher. They put it down and ran to the other side of the plane.

Slumped at the base of a tree lay Demas. He was gagged and tied to the tree. Andrea removed the gag from his mouth. "He looks like he's had a worse beating than Gold," she exclaimed. Dried blood was caked on one side of his head and face. He was unconscious.

Denise felt his neck. "He's still alive."

"What are we going to do?" Andrea asked.

"The radio!" Rainie said. She took the canteen off her shoulder, handed it to Andrea and then took the radio out of her waistband.

"Do you think it will work?" Denise asked.

"It better," Rainie said. "Besides, Mr. McDaniel put new batteries in it and we haven't used it yet."

"Let's climb up there," Denise said and pointed to where the vultures circled above the canyon rim. "It might not broadcast from down here."

They carried Gold over and laid him next to Demas.

"I'll wait with them," Andrea said.

"If he comes to," Rainie said, "don't untie him."

"I won't," she said. "Don't worry." She sat down and poured a little water in her hand for Gold.

Rainie and Denise turned and started climbing out of the canyon. When they reached the canyon rim, the vultures glided through the air about thirty feet above them. They looked like ugly black kites. Rainie could almost imagine she held their strings as they glided over her.

"What are we going to say?" Rainie asked.

"Tell them where we are and that we found the plane."

Rainie turned on the power and then pushed the

broadcast button and spoke into the radio. "Help, we've found the plane crash. We're up San Mateo Canyon. And we have a man who is badly hurt."

Every minute for the next fifteen minutes, Rainie broadcast the same message.

Finally, a voice came over the radio, "Party with the crashed plane, we read you."

Denise and Rainie hugged each other.

"Where up San Mateo are you? Over."

"We're up a side canyon off the main canyon," Rainie spoke into the radio. "The two canyons look like the fork of a snake's tongue."

"Tell them to look for the vultures," Denise interrupted.

Rainie added Denise's message.

"We've got you. Over."

They heard the beating of the helicopter in the east and soon they could see it. The vultures scattered on its approach. Rainie and Denise stepped back closer to the canyon rim as the black helicopter hovered over them. Rainie felt a hard pressure against her chest as the helicopter landed. She held her hat on with one hand.

The door slid open and two uniformed men jumped out. One man had a first aid kit in his hand. "Where's the injured man," he yelled.

Rainie and Denise led them down into the canyon.

"I see you found my radio," the other officer said on the way down.

"Yes, I'm glad we had it just now." Rainie

handed it back to him.

"Thanks." He smiled and said, "I never thought I'd see it again."

16

Reading the Signs

$\mathcal{T}$wo days later, Rainie and Denise sat in the Geronimo Springs Museum meeting room listening to the archaeologist's speech about the Mimbres Indians. At least, Denise was listening. Rainie was having a hard time paying attention. Her mind kept racing back to all that had happened in the past few days.

Rainie still couldn't get the picture out of her mind of Andrea's reunion with her parents. It had to be one of the happiest moments of her life. She was sure it was for Andrea.

Demas was going to survive, but he would probably spend most of the rest of his life in prison. The DEA agents said he'd found the drug plane before the smugglers, buried the pilot, and then covered the plane with branches in an effort to hide it. But the smugglers found Demas before

107

he could transport and sell the drugs. The agents were surprised that the smugglers hadn't killed him.

Gold was going to survive too, but it would be a while before he regained all his strength. Rainie couldn't imagine how the dog had dragged himself all the way back to the cabin and then down to the arroyo to get help for Demas. Now Andrea and her parents planned to adopt Gold.

As the archaeologist closed her speech, Rainie began to worry. Had she and Denise really found something that would help the archaeologist? Maybe she shouldn't have made the appointment after the meeting.

Ten days ago, this had seemed so important to her. Now she realized that there were so many other things in life that were important besides just solving the meaning of the petroglyphs. Those petroglyph signs had seemed so mysterious. And the idea of walking by the Holy Spirit had also seemed confusing and mysterious. Now she understood that she could spend the rest of her life learning to read those mysterious signs. God wouldn't always send her doves or ravens to steer her in the right direction, but she could trust Him on her journey.

When the archaeologist had finished, members of the audience moved forward to shake her hand and to talk with her.

"Shouldn't we go up now?" Denise asked.

"No, I'm going to wait until everyone is gone."

Finally, the last person left. The archaeologist put her notes in her briefcase and said, "Are you the girls I have the appointment with?"

"Yes," Rainie said.

"Grab a chair and come sit down."

Rainie and Denise each took chairs from the front row and brought them to the table next to the podium.

"I've heard a lot about you girls," she said. "I read the article on the front of the Albuquerque paper about how you saved that kidnapped girl's life. I've been wondering what else you discovered."

"I don't think it's much," Rainie said.

"I think what Rainie discovered will really help you," Denise said. Rainie and Denise spread Denise's pictures on the table in front of the archaeologist.

"These are great pictures," she said.

"Thanks," Denise said.

"If Denise hadn't taken them," Rainie said, "we might not have found Andrea. But we wanted to talk with you about the petroglyphs."

Rainie and Denise explained the pictures and what they thought the petroglyphs meant and how they found the rock piles.

"What do you think the rock piles are?" Rainie asked. "Do you think they're graves?"

"No, the Mimbres people didn't bury their dead under rock cairns," she said. "They might be a solar calendar or hunting shrines."

"Are they important finds?" Rainie asked.

"I've heard of other finds like these," she said. "But I believe your interpretation of the petroglyphs may lead me and other archaeologists to many significant discoveries. I already know of other places where there are petroglyphs just like these."

"That's great," Denise said.

"You see, in archaeology we follow things out step by step. You've given us another step that may lead to many wonderful finds."

Rainie smiled and said, "We've been learning to take things one step at a time, too, in the last few weeks."

"Maybe we could end up becoming archaeologists," Denise said.

"Maybe," the archaeologist said. "From the looks of things, you two would be good ones."

Rainie knew that it didn't matter right now what she would become. What mattered was that she had learned to take one step at a time in the Spirit. She wasn't worried about the future. She was excited; because the Christian life is a wonderful adventure, especially when you say yes to Jesus and follow the signs of His leading.

When Rainie and Denise returned to Denise's truck after the meeting, the right front tire was flat. In the dust over the fender someone had written, "Go home or else."

"What did we do?" Rainie asked.

"I don't know," Denise said, "but somebody obviously feels threatened."

"I guess we won't have to search for another mystery," Rainie said, "one has already found us."

Glossary

arroyo—a deep, dry gully in a dry area that usually only fills with water after a recent rain.

bench—a flat area of land that at an earlier time was the shore of a sea or lake or the floodplain of a river.

cairns—a heap of stones piled up as a memorial or as a landmark.

lariat—a long, light rope (made of hemp or leather) used with a running noose to catch livestock or with or without a noose to tie grazing animals.

mesa—a high, wide and flat area of land with sharp, rocky slopes that level down to the surrounding area.

mesquite—a spiny, deep-rooted tree or bush that forms extensive thickets, bears pods rich in sugar, and is important as livestock feed. Commonly found in the southwestern United States and Mexico.

petroglyph—a carving or inscription on a rock.

piñons—a small pine tree, with large edible seeds. Commonly found in western North America.